Hamster Holmes

A BIT STUMPED

By **Albin Sadar**
Illustrated by **Valerio Fabbretti**

Ready-to-Read

Simon Spotlight
New York London Toronto Sydney New Delhi

To Nancy and Jack—A. S.

To Mom and Dad—V. F.

SIMON SPOTLIGHT
An imprint of Simon & Schuster Children's Publishing Division
1230 Avenue of the Americas, New York, New York 10020
This Simon Spotlight edition December 2018
Text copyright © 2018 by Albin Sadar
Illustrations copyright © 2018 by Valerio Fabbretti
All rights reserved, including the right of reproduction in whole or in part in any form.
SIMON SPOTLIGHT, READY-TO-READ, and colophon are registered trademarks
of Simon & Schuster, Inc.
For information about special discounts for bulk purchases, please contact Simon & Schuster
Special Sales at 1-866-506-1949 or business@simonandschuster.com.
Manufactured in the United States of America 1118 LAK
10 9 8 7 6 5 4 3 2 1
This book has been cataloged with the Library of Congress.
ISBN 978-1-5344-2192-9 (hc)
ISBN 978-1-5344-2191-2 (pbk)
ISBN 978-1-5344-2193-6 (eBook)

Hamster Holmes opened
the window in his den.
"It is a beautiful morning
to solve a mystery,"
he said.
Dr. Watt agreed.

Dr. Watt was a firefly.

He blinked his light on and off to talk.

A long flash of light was a dash.

A short flash of light was a dot.

All of a sudden, they heard
a strange ringing sound.
Hamster Holmes jumped.
"What is that?"
he asked Dr. Watt.
Dr. Watt flashed a message.

"Of course, Dr. Watt.
It is the phone!"
Hamster Holmes said,
and he picked it up.
They did not get many
phone calls.

"Good morning,"
said the caller.
"My name is Rufus Feathers.
I need help with a mystery!"
"You have called the right place,"
said Hamster Holmes.

They went straight to the
tree house where Rufus lived.
Rufus showed them the patio he
was building.
It was covered in a design
made of tiles.

"This is a very nice patio,"
Hamster Holmes told Rufus,
"but what happened to the rest
of the tiles?"
"That is the mystery!"
Rufus told him.

Rufus went on.
"I set out the tiles yesterday
and then took a break.
When I came back, most of
the yellow tiles were gone!"

Hamster Holmes and Dr. Watt
looked for clues.
They did not find much at first.
Would this be the first case that
they could not solve?

Then Hamster Holmes found
something that made his
nose twitch.
It was a line in the dirt.
"We will follow it to see
where it takes us,"
he said.

The line stopped at a path
made of bricks that led to
three homes.
"Whoever lives there might be
able to help!"
Hamster Holmes said.

Their friend Corny O'Squirrel
lived in the first house.
"Have you seen any of these tiles?"
Hamster Holmes asked.
Corny had not.
Annie Bunny lived next door.
She had not seen any tiles, either.

Josiah Mutt lived in the third house.

"Have you seen any tiles?"

Hamster Holmes asked.

"I have not seen any towels.

I do not use towels.

I just shake really fast to dry off!"

Josiah said.

Hamster Holmes explained that they

were looking for tiles, not towels.

Josiah had not seen any tiles, either.

Hamster Holmes and Dr. Watt
went back to their den to think
about the clues.
First, they wondered what had
made the line in the dirt.

"Maybe it was a bicycle!"
said Hamster Holmes.
"They have two wheels but make
a single line in dirt."
It was possible,
but they were not sure.

Next, Hamster Holmes wondered,
"Why would someone take only
the yellow tiles?"
Just then a beam of sunlight
came through the window.
It shined off the water bottle and
a vase, and then it hit a tile.

The yellow tile looked even
brighter than before!
That gave Hamster Holmes
an idea.

They went to the park so
Hamster Holmes could run
on the wheel.
It helped him think.
"Aha!" Hamster Holmes
shouted.

"I thought the line in the dirt ended at the brick path," Hamster Holmes told Dr. Watt. "What if the line continues on the other side of the path?"

Sure enough, they found another line in the dirt on the other side of the brick path and followed it. "Now there should be a wheelbarrow nearby," Hamster Holmes said. "It makes a single line and can be used to carry tiles." Dr. Watt spotted one!

They walked over to it and saw
a door in the ground.
"We could not see this home
from the brick path,"
said Hamster Holmes.
"This mystery is solved!"

A little mole named Dougie
opened the door and said,
"I think you are looking for me."
He told them he could not see well,
but he was able to see the yellow tiles
because they were so bright.
He did not know they were part
of a design because he could not
see the darker green or red tiles.

Dougie wished he could give
the tiles back to Rufus,
but he had already used them.
He showed them inside his home.
"They look awesome!"
Rufus said.

Rufus was happy that Dougie
loved the yellow tiles as much
as he did.
Dougie bought new tiles, and then
he, Dr. Watt, and Hamster Holmes
helped Rufus finish the patio!
It was a tough case to solve . . .
but they did it again!

Do you want to solve mysteries like
Hamster Holmes and **Dr. Watt?**
Turn the page for a fun activity
and a special case to solve
with Morse code!

Solve the Mystery!

There is a new mystery to solve, and this time it is your turn to crack the code . . . and the case. It all starts when Ouchy the porcupine, a friend of Hamster Holmes and Dr. Watt, loses his comb . . . again! Hamster Holmes and Dr. Watt split up to look for it. Dr. Watt spots the comb, but it is too heavy for him to carry.

Dr. Watt flashes a message to Ouchy in Morse code . . . but Ouchy does not understand. Can you help Ouchy read the Morse code and solve the mystery?

Check the answer key on the last page of this book when you are ready. You can also use the Morse code chart to write a secret message to a friend.

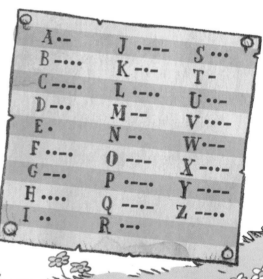

Find the Differences

When Hamster Holmes and Dr. Watt stopped
by the tree house, Dr. Watt did a drawing
of the area. After the detectives left, Rufus
Feathers began to wonder if the missing
yellow tiles were inside his tree house after
all. He took everything out, but he did not
find the tiles . . . until Hamster Holmes and
Dr. Watt solved the case! Rufus cleaned up the
mess and thinks he put everything back in his
house, but he forgot a few things.

Dr. Watt did another drawing of the tree
house to help Rufus find the rest of his
belongings. Can you find the differences
between the two drawings? (Hint: There are
five objects in Drawing B that do not appear
in Drawing A.)

Check the answer key at the back of this book when you are ready.

DRAWING A

DRAWING B

Great job, detective!

Do you want to be a detective?
Here are some fun facts about fingerprints to help you solve your next case:

Are prints only made with fingers?

Even though the word "fingerprints" includes the word "finger," there are other kinds of prints we humans make with our palms and toes and feet. Even the soles of our shoes make prints that can be used to solve a case!

Do animals have fingerprints?

Some animals have fingerprints, including koala bears, chimpanzees, and gorillas. Koala fingerprints are very similar to human fingerprints. Sometimes it can be hard for detectives to tell if a print was made by a human or a koala!

Do twins have matching fingerprints?

Did you know there is one easy way to tell identical twins apart? Even if identical twins wear matching clothes and hairstyles and look exactly alike, each twin will have a unique set of fingerprints!

ANSWER KEY:

Answer to "Solve the Mystery!" on pages 28–29: The comb is at the park!

Answers to "Find the Differences" on pages 30–31: The following items appear in Drawing B but not in Drawing A: a teacup, an alarm clock, a boot, a top hat, and a book.